BY KATHLEEN DOHERTY

ILLUSTRATED BY
CHIP WASS

# DON'T FEED THE BEAR

STERLING CHILDREN'S BOOKS
New York

**Of course, Bear had to have the last word.**

When they had their fill, they put out the fire. The next morning they worked on a new sign.

They chowed down.
After the main course,
they smooshed
marshmallows and chocolate
between graham crackers
for the most
lip-smackin' dessert.

It was the **_perfect picnic._**

The ranger smiled at Bear.
And Bear smiled back.
They both had the same idea.

Later that afternoon,
Bear and the ranger found
quite a surprise.

Piles and piles of goodies!

With their
new signs ready,

it was time to wait.

Bear made
a change.

So did the ranger.

The ranger looked at Bear.

Bear looked at the ranger.

~~DON'T~~ FEED
THE BEAR

(NO MATTER WHAT ~~HE SAYS~~)

A war with words had begun.

It didn't work.

Bear tried a trick.

**The campers stared.
No one fed the ranger.
No one fed Bear.**

# SCRIBBLE, THONK!

Bear put up his own sign.

Bear's tummy rumbled.
He snarled and grumbled.
No more **chewy cookies**?
No more *juicy burgers*?

# STOMPITY, STOMP,
## GRRRRRR!

DON'T FEED
THE BEAR

The ranger was pounding
a sign into the ground.

**Early one morning, Bear heard**

SMACKiTY!
SMACK!
WHOMP!

He clomped off
to investigate.

Mac and cheese . . .
carrot cake . . . meatball stew!

Bear loved when campers left him grub.